illustrated by Jan Pyk

June Rachuy Brindel

LUAP

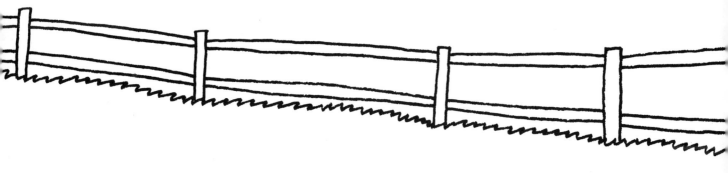

THE BOBBS-MERRILL COMPANY, INC. INDIANAPOLIS NEW YORK

to Paul

This story grew out of material originally written
for radio programs at the National Music Camp,
Interlochen, Michigan.

THE BOBBS-MERRILL COMPANY, INC.
A SUBSIDIARY OF HOWARD W. SAMS & CO., INC.
PUBLISHERS   INDIANAPOLIS   KANSAS CITY   NEW YORK
Text copyright © 1971 by June Rachuy Brindel
Illustrations copyright © 1971 by Jan Pyk
Design by Jack Jaget
Printed in the United States of America
Library of Congress catalog card number: 75-156108
0 9 8 7 6 5 4 3 2 1

Very strange things happened to Luap. Stranger things happened to Luap than had ever happened to anyone else in the history of Salamander City. He would be strolling along in the usual way, when all of a sudden he would find himself upside down, walking on his fingertips! Grocery money would get lost in worm holes and old soup cans. His mother didn't like that.

Other strange things happened too. One day Luap would see with his fingers. The next day he would taste with his ears. Luap's father didn't like that. "That's not the way it's done!" he would shout. "You're going to get into trouble."

He was right. Luap did get into trouble—on the day he started to think with his stomach.

It happened, of all places, in school, which is not the best place to be when your brain doesn't work.

"Luap," said Miss Pepperitch, "please recite the 'Thirty Days Hath.' "

Luap cleared his throat. Suddenly he felt light in the head and very excited in the stomach.

"Well?" said Miss Pepperitch, tapping her foot.

" 'Thirty days hath . . .' " Luap paused. His brain fluttered like a bird let loose.

> *"Thirty days hath spaghetti,*
> *Pumpkin pie and apple betty,*
> *All the rest have chocolate cone,*
> *Except lollipop alone—"*

"*What!*" gasped Miss Pepperitch.

Luap held his breath. He could hear his stomach going on with the silly rhyme.

> *"Which has toasted ice cream cheese*
> *But at breakfast French fried peas!"*

Miss Pepperitch was breathing very fast. Suddenly her heels started clicking, and Luap felt himself being marched down the hall to the Principal's office.

The Principal knew everything about boys, but he could not figure out what was wrong with Luap. Luap's parents knew everything about stomachs, but they could not figure out what was wrong either. So they called in the Experts.

The Experts all had different ideas. One thought Luap was eating too much and advised starving. Another thought he was not eating enough and advised stuffing. Luap's mother tried both. Some days Luap was fat and some days he was thin. But it didn't stop his stomach from thinking. "One peach and one pineapple equal two cans of parsley soup," he would say. Or " 'Twas the night before elephant marmalade."

"Until he learns to use his head," cried the Principal, "he can't go back to class!"

Luap went off and hid in the empty lot behind the greenhouse. He didn't want to see anyone. He just sat and looked at a clump of cockleburs.

Suddenly a nose the shape of a cocklebur appeared, then two sparkling black eyes, a crinkly face, and an elflike body.

"Are you cabbaging?" asked a strange little man.

Luap couldn't believe his ears. Then he saw the little man whirl around and start to walk on his fingertips!

Luap had not done that since his stomach started thinking. He whirled upside down so fast that his shoes flew off and landed in the cottonwood tree.

"I'll radish them for you," cried the little man. He took a deep breath and blew it out at the ground with great force, spurting himself up like a rocket. In one second he had grabbed the shoes and whistled them onto Luap's feet.

"Sausage you to the rotten stump!" shouted the little man.

Away they both went on their fingertips. The little man could do anything. He could jump six feet into the air and twirl like a pinwheel. He could count the hairs on a fly's leg. He could even count backwards from infinity to nothing (he said). Besides that, he could skip on his ears, play drums with his small toes, and perform millions of other tricks, some of which Luap learned.

Finally they were both so tired they collapsed on a heap of dry grass.

"This is fun," said Luap. "But it gets me into trouble."

"How?"

Luap told the little man all about the lost grocery money, the stomach rhymes, and his problems at school. The little man screeched with anger and exploded.

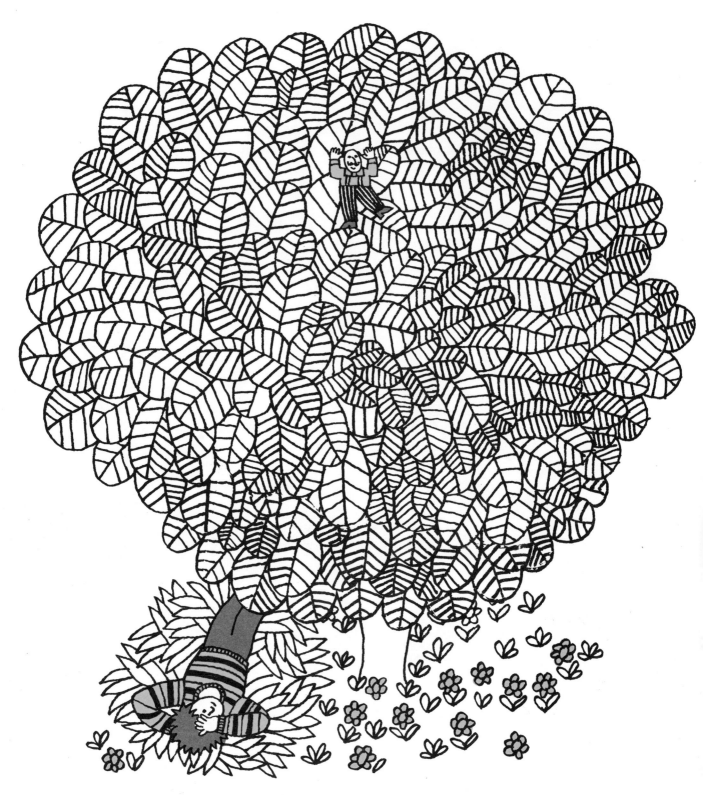

Luap looked around for him and saw him perched on top of the cottonwood, clicking his teeth very fast and making frightful faces in all directions.

"What's the matter?" called Luap.

"I'm going to teach that bunch a lesson!"

"How?"

But the little man did not answer. He simply started spinning and shot straight upward out of sight.

Instantly the sky shivered and lightning squealed through the trees. Luap felt himself whirled about and thrown down onto his feet. Everything became very strange, and Luap ran home as fast as he could and hid in a closet.

Suddenly he heard excited voices. He opened the door and saw his mother and father standing on their fingertips!

Luap gasped. "What are you doing?"

"The whole town's bewitched!" shouted Father. "Everyone is upside down!"

"Except you," said Mother suspiciously. "Don't you feel a little bit like—flipping over, son?"

"Not a bit."

"How do we get down?" demanded Father.

Luap gulped. "I don't know."

Father was angry. "Stop playing tricks and get us down on our feet!"

"Please, dear," said Mother.

"But I'm not doing it," said Luap. "Honest."

"Then who is?"

Luap considered. "I think I know. But I don't know if I can find him."

"Scurry out and look," urged Father.

"Does it hurt?" whispered Luap.

"Surprisingly enough"—Mother smoothed up her apron—"it's quite comfortable, though how it could be I can't imagine."

But Father had started shouting again. So Luap left hurriedly to look for the little man.

Outside, the town was in a turmoil. Everyone except Luap was up-side down. Bus drivers, construction workers, babies, doctors, policemen, robbers were all walking on their fingertips. Some were also singing with their noses. Others were talking with their ears.

Cars were stalled because the drivers couldn't get their feet down to the gas pedals. Elevators went up when you pushed the down button and down when you pushed the up button. Telephones gave off smells instead of sounds. Everything was a mess.

Wherever Luap walked, people turned to stare, to point, to whisper to their neighbors, and finally to follow, until the whole town was trailing after him, like rats after the Pied Piper.

"Look at him standing on his feet!" someone shouted. "How does he do it?"

"I think he's the one responsible for this!" screamed a nasty voice.

"He must be! He's the only one who can walk right side up. Let's get him!" The crowd started closing in. Closer and closer came the waving, threatening feet and the yelling faces, until Luap was surrounded.

Just then a sharp high voice rang out over the noise. "Stop this immediately!"

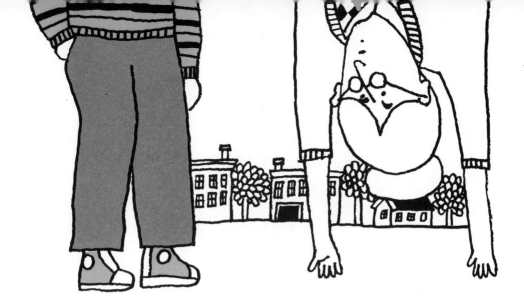

Luap looked down into the mouth of Miss Pepperitch. "Aren't you ashamed?" she cried to the people. They grew quiet. "Now, then, Luap, do you know the cause of this catastrophe?"

Luap gulped. "No, but I think I know someone who does."

"Let us at him!" yelled the crowd.

Luap looked pleadingly down at Miss Pepperitch. "I don't think he will talk to me if there are others around."

"I see," said Miss Pepperitch, understanding. She looked at Luap with a friendliness she had never shown before. Then, turning to the people, she said, "You may go now." And they did!

Luap was awestruck. Never had Miss Pepperitch seemed so majestic. She was like a queen. "Maybe it's good for her to be upside down," he thought.

"Now, then, Luap," she said calmly, with not a hair out of place, "about this person. Apparently he knows a very powerful secret." She winked. "However," she looked at Luap severely, "you must make him realize that this can't go on! The town's not set up for it—I mean set down."

Luap nodded.

Miss Pepperitch smiled. "It's all right for it to happen once in a while, to one person at a time . . ." She paused and looked at him. "But to a whole city—it will never do! Do you understand?"

"Yes'm," gulped Luap. "I think so."

"Very well, then, see your—uh, friend—immediately." And she marched away, tinkling as she went, for she had put thimbles on all her fingers to keep her nails clean.

Luap dashed out to the empty lot and looked high and low through the cockleburs, but there was no sign of the little man. He wasn't in the cottonwood tree, or on the pile of dry grass, or in the worm holes or the giant black-eyed Susans. Luap sat down on some old soup cans. He was very discouraged. He put his elbow on his knee and his chin on his hand and stared glumly at the white cottony head of an old dandelion.

"Oh, phoo!" he said. The dandelion feathers flew in all directions. And along with them flew something crinkly and very small—and strangely familiar. Luap caught it in his hand and looked straight into the face of the little man!

"Olleh!" said a very tiny voice.

"Gee!" breathed Luap, blowing the little man up into the air again.

"Hey!"

"Sorry," said Luap, catching him. "I'd better look away when I talk to you."

"Indeed you had!"

"But why are you so small?"

"I feel that way," the little man said. "I'm as big as I feel."

Luap was overwhelmed with admiration. "Gee!" he breathed again, quickly turning away as he did. "You can do anything!"

The little man instantly became the size of a coconut. Luap was so surprised that he dropped him. The little man got up indignantly and dusted off his clothes. He began to grow rapidly until he was as tall as the cottonwood tree. Then he looked down at Luap. "You don't seem pleased. Why?"

Luap hesitated. "It's not a bad idea once in a while, but—" Luap looked up timidly. "But not everyone at once. The town's not set up for it! I mean set down."

"Gratitude!"

"I'm sorry," said Luap. "But, you see, some things work better right side up. Elevators and buses and—"

"Nonsense!" growled the little man. "Anyway, it's out of my hands now." And he started to walk away.

"Wait!" cried Luap. "Can't you stop it?"

"Hmph!" said the little man. He was shrinking again and had reached the size of a blueberry bush. "They can stop it themselves if they're smart enough." He continued to shrink as he walked.

"How?" called Luap. But the little man kept shrinking until there was nothing left of him, and a voice about as loud as a mosquito whispered in Luap's ear, "Perspective!"

That was all.

Luap did not know what "perspective" meant. He decided to find Miss Pepperitch and ask her.

Everybody in town was still fingering around like mad, shrieking at the bottoms of their lungs. Luap tried to keep out of sight. Finally he found Miss Pepperitch standing on her head on her desk, putting it in order. She listened carefully to what he said, and when he got to the part about "perspective," she said, *"Aha!"*

"What does it mean?" asked Luap.

"It means," said Miss Pepperitch, "that there is more than one way of looking at things." And as she said it, *whoosh!* she whirled around and landed on her feet.

"That's the key to the mystery!" she cried. "The Mayor must be informed." She put on her hat. "Come, Luap. It is our civic duty."

People stared up at them as they passed. Crowds parted to let them by. At the City Hall, they went straight to the office of the Mayor, who was talking wildly and waving his foot at his assistants. "How do you do it?" he gasped, when he saw Luap and Miss Pepperitch.

"This boy has the answer," Miss Pepperitch said. "Tell him, Luap."

"Well, sir," said Luap. "It's just that things look a little different from different angles."

The Mayor looked Luap down and up. He looked his assistants up and down. "You're right!" he shouted, and *whoosh!* he whirled around and landed on his feet. Immediately he pushed down all the buttons on his desk. "Call the reporters!" he yelled. "Get me the Chief of Police!"

Luap and Miss Pepperitch huddled in a corner out of the way of the twirling arms and legs while one person after another discovered the key to the mystery. All over the city, as the news spread, people flipped back on their feet. Soon everyone was standing upright again and life was going on much as it always had.

Except for certain changes.

Luap was back in school, but no one minded when he thought with his stomach or walked on his fingertips.

And on Saturday afternoons in the park one could sometimes see the Principal riding backwards on his bicycle.

Miss Pepperitch redecorated her classroom and hung a sign over the blackboard reading: